What do the grown-ups do?

Richard the Vet

"What makes these books noteworthy are the practical details from the mouths of the real workers, which fascinate rather than bore. It's eye-opening stuff."
Teach Primary magazine.

"To say that I was totally enamoured by the 'What do' series is something of an understatement. I always feel that the ultimate test lies in how one's own children treat such reading materials. When I asked them, if they were enjoying the books, they were unequivocal in their praise of them. In fact our daughter even lent 'Papa' to next door's children but popped back within three days to request its immediate return! On such evidence, I have to state that Mairi McLellan, the author, has managed to achieve a level of literary 'magic' that perhaps only the good Dr Seuss (Theodore Geisel) might have mastered many years earlier than she."
Pocketful of Rye.

"This series is a great way of demystifying the grown-ups' world for children. I look forward to the next few titles."
Primary Times (Avon).

"An informative and fun way to introduce your children to the world of living."
Gordon Buchanan, Wildlife Filmmaker.

"Really detailed and informative books, which contain exactly the questions that intelligent children ask, and adults are often unable to answer. There is fun, humour and a wonderful sense of place too."
Dr Ken Greig, Rector, Hutchesons' Grammar School.

What do the grown-ups do?

Richard the Vet

Mairi McLellan

Matador
9 Priory Business Park
Kibworth Beauchamp
Leicestershire LE8 0RX, UK
Tel: (+44) 116 279 2299
Fax: (+44) 116 279 2277
Email: books@troubador.co.uk
Web: www.troubador.co.uk/matador

ISBN: 978 1783065 264

Editor: Eleanor MacCannell

British Library Cataloguing in Publication Data.
A catalogue record for this book is available from the British Library.

Matador is an imprint of Troubador Publishing Ltd

www.kidseducationalbooks.com

What do the grown-ups do?

Dear Reader,

What do the grown-ups do? is a series of books designed to educate children about the workplace using chatty, light-hearted stories, written through the eyes of the children.

The aim is to offer the children an insight into adult working life, to stimulate their thinking and to help motivate them to learn more about the jobs that interest them. Perhaps by introducing these concepts early, we can broaden their ideas for the future as well as increase their awareness of the world around them. It's just a start and at this age, although the message is serious, it is designed to be fun.

For younger children who will be doing a combination of reading and being read to, these books will be reasonably challenging. I have deliberately tried not to over-simplify them too much in order to maintain reality, whilst making them fun to enjoy.

The books can be read in any order but they are probably best starting from the beginning. The order of the series can be found at the back of this book. Many more will be coming soon so please check the website for updates: **www.kidseducationalbooks.com**.

I hope you enjoy them.

Happy reading!

Mairi

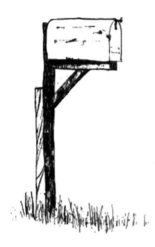

A note of thanks to Richard, who is truly passionate about his job, who is always first out and last in on his windsurfer, and a better brother-in-law you could not meet (aside from my other, equally lovely brothers-in-law, of course!). Also to Richard's vet practice, Parkside Vets, their clients for letting me visit their farms and animals, Balgay Farm and of course, my parents - thank you!

Life by the sea in Badaneel

The Mackenzie girls, Ava, Skye and Gracie, lived in a beautiful village by the sea, called Badaneel. Life in the Northwest Highlands was one big adventure, surrounded by fresh air, beaches and mountains.

Views around Badaneel.

It was the October holidays and the girls were just back from a trip to the Isle of Tiree, the most westerly island of the Inner Hebrides of Scotland. Tiree had even more beaches than Badaneel!

Skye surfing in Tiree.

The island is a famous windsurfing destination because it has beaches all around it, so no matter which way the wind blows, there is always a beach where it is blowing in the right direction. It is also good for waves, which means fun for the windsurfers, surfers, boogieboarders, kitesurfers and paddleboarders!

Ava boogieboarding.

The Mackenzie family was on holiday with their Auntie Fee, Uncle Richard and their cousins, Molly and Pete. The children were in and out the water all day and Ava thought it was the best holiday ever!

Lessons from the windsurfing instructor.

Of particular excitement was their first windsurfing lesson on the Tiree loch. The girls were just old enough to start learning as the twins, Ava and Skye, were six and Gracie was five. Tiree had an amazing little loch, with shallow water, which was perfect for learning. After a little instruction on the shore, the girls were up and off. It was hard work but great fun!

Gracie and Skye windsurfing on the loch.

Windsurfing was a great sport for all the family. In the lighter winds, the Mackenzie girls could windsurf on the loch and when the heavier wind came in, Mother and Uncle Richard got to play in the sea!

Mother and Uncle Richard having fun in the waves!

Richard blasting on his windsurfer!

Ava with her boogieboard.

Uncle Richard flies a kite with the kids.

Gracie pulls her board upwind.

Uncle Richard cooks sausages on the BBQ.

Jobs

Back in Badaneel, it was time to catch up on some of the jobs that needed doing. Mother said that it was important to have fun, but it was also important to work hard. After a week of holiday, Mother and Father had a lot of work to catch up on, and so did the Mackenzie girls!

Today was Saturday and they were down at the Badaneel stables, working with the horses. There was a lot to be done to help the owner, including polishing the tack, mucking out the stables, grooming and so on. Every Saturday they spent two hours working at the stables, and at the end they were allowed to ride the horses. It was a good deal as they enjoyed working with the horses, and the owner taught them how to ride and how to care for the ponies. At the end of the day there was a tuck shop for those who worked hard!

Gracie and Skye exercise the ponies.

The girls were exercising and feeding the ponies when Gracie noticed that one wasn't eating well. The owner had a look and decided to call the vet. The Mackenzie girls always found it funny when the vet came as it was their uncle, Richard, who treated the horses when they were ill.

Richard the Vet

Richard the vet.

"Hi Uncle Richard!" shouted the Mackenzie girls, as he pulled up in his car. "Hi girls!" he shouted back, as he gathered his vet equipment. The girls thought Uncle Richard was great fun. He was always up for a game of rounders on the beach, or kite flying, but his favourite sport was windsurfing. When they were in Tiree, Richard was always last out the water, and often windsurfed until it was dark! Today, like the Mackenzie girls, he was back to work.

Uncle Richard loved his work and he loved animals. "What have you got for me today, girls?" he asked as he headed into the stables. "Foxy the pony has a sore mouth I think," said Ava, pointing to the little black pony that was sniffing inside Richard's car.

"Let's go and have a look, shall we?" said Richard, as he got a bucket of feed to tempt the pony into the stall. "Excuse me, Richard," said Gracie, with her best manners. "We are investigating grown-up jobs with Mama. So far we've seen a fisherman, a stockfarmer, an actor and a doctor. Could we watch you work to see what a vet does, please?" she asked.

"Of course! I'd be delighted!" said Richard laughing. "It's great to see you so keen to learn about jobs. I have a couple of customers after this one. Would you like to join me for the rest of the afternoon and I can show you around?"

"Yes please!" shouted the Mackenzie girls in unison.

"Great, I'll call your mum to check if it's okay. In the meantime, let's see what's wrong with this pony's mouth," he said.

"It's always easier to use the carrot rather than the stick approach, if possible," said Richard, as the pony made its way calmly to its stable. "As vets, we try to prevent the animals from getting stressed. By leading them in gently, we keep them calm, while we assess what is wrong with them. In this case, I have a fairly good idea of the problem, as the last time I visited I noticed that she might need her tooth out. I don't take teeth out until it is absolutely necessary, but I fear that this time it might be."

Richard tempts the pony to the stall with some food.

Richard got the pony into the stable and held it tight.

"When I am treating animals, I try to make them as comfortable as possible. They don't like us prodding about inside their mouths, especially if we need to remove teeth! Vets have developed a system to try to minimise how stressed the horses and ponies get," smiled Richard. "First, we sedate the animal with this jab, or jag, as we call it in Scotland. This makes them sleepy and numbs their senses, so they feel less pain.

Foxy is sedated with a jag.

"The next step is to get what we call the *head stand* and *stockman's gag*. These hold the pony's head in place, with its mouth fixed open, so that we can get a look inside. The head stand and the stockman's gag are the vet's friend – as long as they work!" laughed Richard. "There are times when they collapse and the end result is a very sore hand!"

Richard calmly manoeuvred the stockman's gag over the horse's nose. It was a big metal contraption with bits that went inside the horse's mouth. Under the horse's chin was the headstand, used to keep the chin up so that Richard could look inside the mouth.

"It looks rather uncomfortable!" said Gracie.

"It's better than having a very sore mouth with a rotten tooth!' replied Richard. "I'm afraid there is no easier way to deal with the problem."

The pony gets the stockman's gag fitted.

Richard had a look inside the horse's mouth. "This pony has two rotten teeth and ulcers, both of which will be causing her a great deal of pain. Her teeth also have lots of sharp edges, which need filing down," he explained to the owner and the girls.

The owner nodded. "She's not been well eating for some time. I knew something was wrong."

Richard inspects the pony's mouth.

"Would you like to have a look, girls?" asked Richard as he held Foxy's mouth open. Ava, Skye and Gracie moved forwards slowly to have a closer look. They were used to dealing with horses and ponies, but they had never looked right inside a horse's mouth.

"Yuk!" shouted Ava, as she jumped back from the pony. "You mustn't shout, Ava," said Richard, calmly. "It frightens the horses and we don't want to upset them." Ava apologised. She knew better but the horse's mouth was not a pretty sight. The teeth were all black, the mouth was full of bits of chewed grass and it was generally rather disgusting!

Foxy's mouth.

"What's next, Uncle Richard?" asked Skye.

"We need to get the equipment to remove the rotten teeth. I have a tool, which is like a massive pair of pliers, and the job is simply to wriggle the tooth until I can pull it out. It is very important not to break the teeth!"

Richard works at removing the rotten tooth.

Richard gently moved the tooth until is was loose enough to pull it out. "There we go!" he said, as he gave Foxy a pat on the neck. "One done, one more to go."

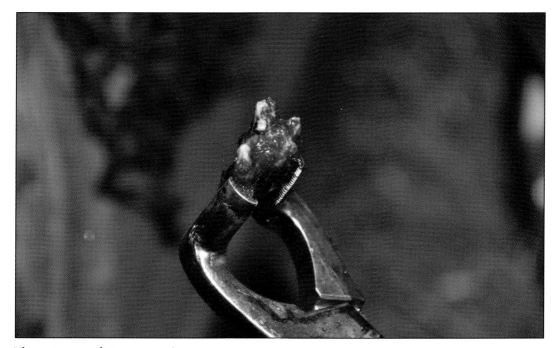

The rotten tooth is removed!

It was quite physical work trying to get the tooth out. He used a rubber band to make sure the grip was held.

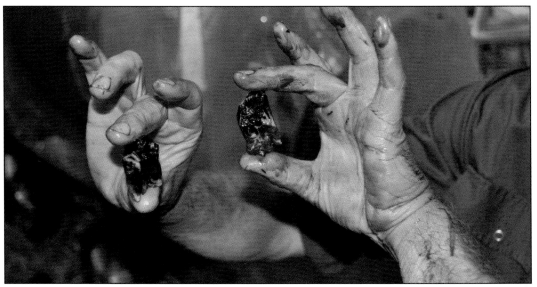

Both teeth removed!

"Excellent," said Richard as he inspected the teeth. "Foxy is going to be much more comfortable now and will soon be back to eating her food as normal."

"Does it bother you getting covered in blood and saliva from the horse's mouth?" asked Skye.

 12

"No, not at all," said Richard. "Our job is to help the animals. Getting covered in blood can be part of that, depending on what needs to be done. When you know that you are doing something for the good of the animal, you just get on with it," he smiled.

"We haven't quite finished here yet, girls," he said. "In treatments such as this, we need to make sure that the animal's mouth does not get infected. To do this, we give them a dose of antibiotics, which helps prevent infection. We also give them painkillers to keep them comfortable as the wound heals. Now we are done!" he said smiling.

The owner thanked Richard as he and the Mackenzie girls tidied up and headed back to the car. "Where to now?" asked Gracie.

"Now we have to travel to see another client, so we have time for a chat about a vet's job on the way, if you like?" said Richard as they headed off down the road. It was a beautiful autumn day in Badaneel and the colours on the leaves gave a warm glow on the hillside. Not a bad day for a drive, thought Ava, and this vet business is all very interesting!

Autumn hills around Badaneel.

"Do you like your job, Richard?" asked Gracie.

"I absolutely love it!" smiled Richard. "I enjoy so many aspects of it – working with the animals, building up good communication with clients and meeting lots of different, interesting people. I love the variety of dealing with different animals with different problems. As vets we are part of a team, but we work most of the time alone and I enjoy the independence and responsibility of this way of working," he said. "I also enjoy being able to work outside. Just look at these amazing views! Every day I am outside, working with animals and every day is a different challenge. It's a great job," he smiled.

Views around Badaneel.

"Are there any parts of the job that you don't like?" asked Ava.

"Like any job, there are good bits and bad bits. Vets typically work very long hours. As animals can get sick at any time, we get calls day or night, with the worst ones being between 3 and 5am!" he laughed. "The most important thing is to have a passion for what you do. We tend to work between 40 to 60 hours per week, but I would rather work 70 hours doing a job I loved than 40 hours doing a job I hated!" he smiled. "When you enjoy your job, it doesn't feel like hard work, even though it might be tiring. Being a vet is quite a selfish existence. It's a morally decent job and we are seen to be helping out, which we are, but we enjoy it! This is all fine when you are a bachelor and have plenty time. However, when you have a family it is harder as you don't get to spend as much time with them as you might like. So, I guess we get to do what we love and people always thank us for helping, but the downside is you are missing out on helping with the family, more so than some other lines of work."

"Do you mostly work with horses?" asked Skye.

"Well, yes and no!" said Richard, smiling. "I am what we call a *big animal vet*. Yes, I work with horses a great deal and our practice or company is very experienced in equine problems. Equine is just another word for something to do with horses. We are busy throughout the year on the equine side. However, I also work on farms, mostly with cattle and sheep. Springtime is extremely busy as I help with calving and lambing. I perform quite a lot of *caesarean sections*, which occur if a mother can't give birth to her calf naturally. A caesarean section is an operation where we need to cut open the cow's belly to let the calf out, otherwise both the calf and the

Most calves and lambs are born in springtime.

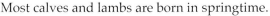

mother can die. Winter is also a busy time on farms as many cattle are kept in sheds. The sheds shelter them from the cold, but can also lead to an increase in disease, as an illness can spread through a shed much more easily than out on the hill. I work with farmers throughout the year to help them manage the *herd health plan*, which is simply a plan that we work on together to ensure that the animals are kept in the best possible health. The health plan involves disease monitoring, vaccines, feeding advice, worm and liver fluke control and so on," said Richard.

Aberdeen Angus cattle wintering in the shed.

"What other types of vets are there?" asked Ava.

"Vets can do a wide variety of different jobs, but there are ten main types.

"*Small animal vets* deal mainly with the care of household pets, such as cats, dogs, rabbits, hamsters and guinea pigs. The full name for a vet is *veterinary surgeon*. We are called surgeons because we often have to operate on animals, kind of like a surgeon in a hospital but not on people!" smiled Richard. "Small animal vets perform operations, x-rays and vaccinations, as well as treat lameness, sore eyes, sore ears, and so on.

"Small animal veterinary surgeons are the most common type of vet in the UK.

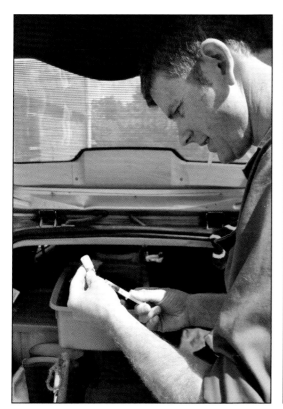

Richard gives Fergus the puppy a vaccine to prevent it from getting ill.

The vaccine is given with a needle.

"A *large animal vet* focuses on the health and productivity of a group of large animals, as well as individual animals. Large animal vets typically work as part of a farm team, responsible for managing the herd health plan, treating disease and balancing nutrition (what they eat). Large animals include cattle, sheep, pigs, or even llamas! For each type of animal, there are many different types of breed. For example a sheep is not simply a sheep; there are Suffolks, Texels, Blackfaces, Mules, and so on. Each breed has different characteristics and, with experience, we learn what to look out for, and how to best manage their health.

Sheep and cattle farm by Point Beach.

"The variety in the job is great fun and challenging. On some farms, we work with prize bulls and cows, which are worth a lot of money, so ensuring they are kept in best possible health is essential. Other places we work at might include animal sanctuaries, where abandoned animals are looked after by volunteers. In these cases, we pop by as often as we can to lend a hand. Each day is different.

A 2-year-old prize Shorthorn bull.

The donkey sanctuary.

"Equine veterinary surgeons are specially trained to treat horses. Horses are different in many ways to other domestic animals and that is why many horse owners prefer to use the services of an equine vet when their horse is

sick or injured. Large animal vets often manage both equine and other large animals but it depends on the speciality of the practice. In our practice, we have a dedicated small animal vet team as well as a dedicated equine team who also attend farms.

"An *exotic animal vet* takes extra training to treat exotic animals, such as ferrets, small rodents, iguanas, turtles, snakes and lizards. Like an equine vet, an exotic vet first trains as a general vet and then studies for further qualifications in their speciality. Vets specialising in the treatment of exotic animals are likely to be found working in private practices, as well as in zoos and even the circus!

"*Avian vets* specialise in treating birds, and can be found working in private practices, zoos and bird sanctuaries. After completing their general veterinary training, this type of vet will undertake specialist training in the care and treatment of birds.

"There are a number of other types of vets that you might find working in the UK today and they include: *feline vets*, who specialise in the care of kittens and cats; *cardiology vets*, who study an animal's heart; *dental vets*, who take care of your pet's teeth; and *marine vets*, who care for animals in the sea.

"There are also *research vets* who work in laboratories where they try to find better ways to treat animals, either through medicine or surgery. Laboratories, zoos, circuses, racetracks, colleges, universities and government agencies all employ vets.

"Right! We have nearly arrived at our destination! This time we are here to float some teeth! Who know what that means?" asked Richard.

The Mackenzie girls shook their heads. "Take them swimming?" laughed Ava. They all laughed. "Not exactly!" smiled Richard, as he got out of the car and headed over to the stables. The Mackenzie girls had barely had a chance to look around by the time Richard had sedated the horse, got him in the stockman's gag and head stand, examined the teeth and was in the process of preparing a bunch of tools in hot soapy water.

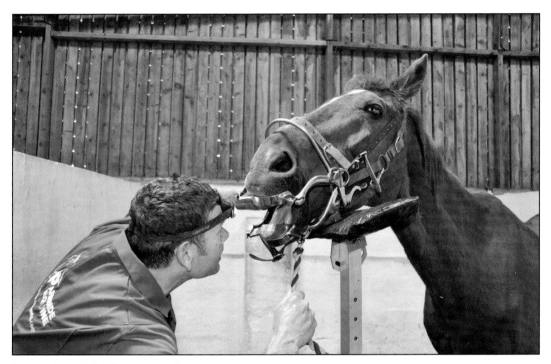

Inspection of the horse's teeth.

Preparation of the tools for the job.

Hot soapy water to clean the tools.

"That was quick!" said Skye, watching Richard going back and forward. "What is in the bucket?"

"These are floats," said Richard. "Floats are like files used to grind down teeth and there are lots of different types. The problem with horse teeth is that they never stop growing, although the growth slows down as they get older. Horses that live in the wild eat for about 18 hours per day. They chew things like trees, bark, dry grasses and so on, which helps keep their teeth filed down. However, in captivity, they get special food, which is often softer. They also do less continuous grazing or eating, so the teeth grow into sharp points. If a horse loses a tooth, the other tooth opposite it has nothing to grind on. If it is not filed, it can grow so much that it stabs the opposite gum!"

"Euwwww! Ouch!" said Ava, grimacing. "Indeed," said Richard.

"Now, just to make things a little tricky, we have to watch that we don't file the teeth *too* much, otherwise we get into raw tissue, which would be very painful for the horse."

"Hmmm," nodded Skye, thinking this was starting to get a little more complicated than she first thought.

"When filing, we can use manual floats or electric power floats. If we use power floats, we must also be careful that they don't get too hot or it will burn the horse's mouth. Lots to watch out for, isn't there?" he smiled. The Mackenzie girls nodded.

Richard with his float, ready to file!

Pointed teeth!

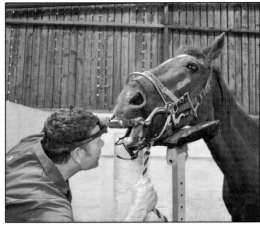
Richard inspects the horse's mouth.

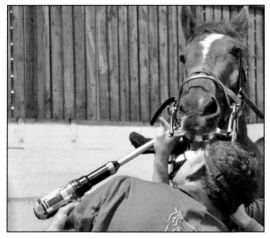
The power float files the teeth.

With his headtorch, Richard can see inside!

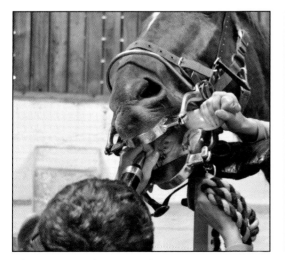
The tongue is held out the way.

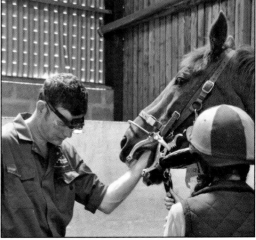
Richard does a final check.

Before long, all the teeth had been filed and the horses were left to settle down in peace. Richard cleaned his equipment, said cheerio to the owner and headed off with the Mackenzie girls to see his next client.

"Do you ever get hurt by the animals?" asked Gracie.

"Sometimes! Thankfully, the more I learn, the less I get hurt. By working with experienced vets over the years, I have learnt how to approach them, where to stand and so on. However, you must always be careful and if possible, try to keep the animals calm. By learning how to handle the animals properly, injuries are kept to a minimum. A good tip when working at the bottom end, with cattle and horses, is to stand very close to their back legs. This stops them kicking you so hard!"

"The bottom end?" laughed Gracie. "You mean like working with their bottom?" At this point all the Mackenzie girls were in stitches. Richard smiled, "Yes, yes, very funny. That is exactly what I mean and you three little rascals are about to see some horse bottoms at my next client." The Mackenzie girls were silenced. This might prove to be rather disgusting, thought Ava. Having said that, nothing could be more disgusting than those maggots she had seen with Papa the Stockfarmer. How bad could it be?

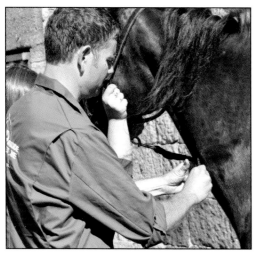

They arrived at a lovely farm with lots of stables. As with the other visits, Richard knew what he was here to do and he quickly had things organised, starting with a sedative to calm the horse before treatment. The horse was taken inside and tied to stop it moving about. The Mackenzie girls hovered nearby, but not so close that they might get kicked!

A sedative is given to the horse.

Ava had suspected that Richard was not joking about working with the horse's bottom, and sure enough, it was time for a bottom inspection. Skye and Gracie looked on, studying the equipment that Richard had brought with him. Richard explained that the horse had a sore bottom and he needed to look inside. He had various tubes, which he looked through to see what the problem might be.

Bottom inspections with the headtorch.

Thankfully, the bottom inspection was soon over. Richard spent quite a lot of time washing things out. He said it was very important to keep good hygiene to prevent disease and infection. Gracie thought this was all quite a good idea and she would have done the same if she had to stick her hand up a horse's bottom!

"Do you mind having to stick your hand up the horse's bottom?" asked Skye.

"Not at all," said Richard, smiling. "I don't even think about it anymore. It's just something we need to do if we are to find out what is wrong with the horse. You get used to it. Now come on! We have a horse with a sore leg to deal with!" he smiled. "Come and meet Buster. He is a sixteen year old with multiple lameness issues. I think you'll like him."

Washing the equipment.

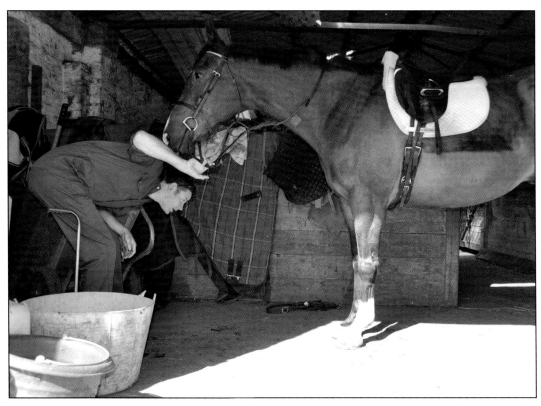

Richard inspects Buster's legs.

It was an exhausting business, thought Gracie. The Mackenzie girls watched as the horse was taken around the ring, walked up and down the courtyard, and inspected in various ways. Richard said he needed to see how he was on his feet in different situations, to try to isolate the problem. The girls liked Buster – he was a very friendly horse.

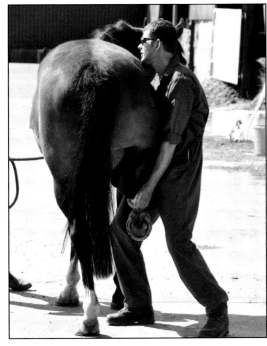

Richard does various tests on the leg.

"How do you fix a lame leg, Richard?" asked Gracie.

"It depends what is wrong with it. This leg is not broken, so it won't require an operation. Buster has *arthritis*, which is inflammation of the joints. Inflammation is when you get heat, swelling and importantly, pain. We can treat this with medicines to reduce and stop the inflammation. Sometimes we inject medicines straight into a horse's joint. However, we must also try to use as many natural-based medicines as we can to help the joints in the leg recover. Buster will be okay. We've done some exercises and given him some joint supplements to help loosen his stiff leg."

Richard watches how Buster walks to check his legs.

Richard continued working with the owner to help other horses, while the Mackenzie girls chatted to him.

Richard inspects the other horses on the farm.

"How do you become a vet?" asked Skye.

"To become a vet, you need to attend an accredited college of veterinary medicine and earn a Doctor of Veterinary Medicine degree. There is a short supply of schools, so getting accepted can be extremely competitive.

"Vet schools are very interested in your academic performance, so you need to work hard at school to get top grades. In addition to this, they also favour applicants who have real work experience. It's very important to try to get a job or internship in a veterinary office during school holidays or weekends, or try to get work on farms, especially at lambing and calving time, or help at your local stables. Keep in touch with your local vet office and see if you can watch what they are doing and help out in any way. Any experience you gain will increase your chance of getting into vet school. Like any job in life, you need to show that you are committed and willing to work hard. Work experience can mean the difference between getting into vet school or not.

"Once you have graduated as a vet, you then work as an assistant vet for 10 to 15 years until you are very confident and capable of working on your own. From there, you can either set up on your own, with your own vet business, or join an existing vet practice, where the business is run and owned by a group of partners, and work your way up to partner," explained Richard.

Ava, Skye and Gracie watched and chatted as Richard worked. He was very busy!

Richard prepares an injection.

Finally, they said cheerio to Buster and went on to visit various other farms. The work was indeed very varied and they met a collie puppy called Torr, who needed a vaccine; a pony called Louis who had a dry skin problem on his head; some sheep who were getting scanned to see whether they were carrying lambs – and the biggest tractor they had ever seen!

Torr the collie puppy.

Louis the pony.

Blackie sheep ready to be scanned.

The girls helped Richard where they could and chatted to all the different owners. They had a great time playing with Torr the puppy, climbing around the sheep pen and inspecting the tractor. Soon it was time to head back. Richard called them over and they all got back into the car.

A massive tractor!   Richard packs up to go home.

The Mackenzie girls had enjoyed a great day. "So, girls," said Richard, "what do you think about being a vet?"

"You get to spend time with lots of different animals," said Gracie, "and help them get better. You meet lots of nice people and chat to them, and you are never bored because every farm has different things that need to be done," she said.

"Yes," said Ava, "but you do have to stick your hand up the bottoms of the animals sometimes, and that is a bit yucky!" she laughed. Richard laughed too. "I'd say that's a pretty good summary. I really love my job, but before you decide to become a vet, you need to be clear of the work involved. Many vets provide emergency care, meaning that we need to be available on nights and weekends. We work a lot of overtime, which means that we work a lot of hours each week. With any job you do, you need to think about the impact that it will have on your personal life as you consider your occupation. Being a vet can be very rewarding, but it is not a career for everyone," said Richard.

The Mackenzie girls thought that being a vet seemed like a great job, and throughout their visits they had learned that work doesn't feel like work if you enjoy it. They all loved animals and they liked the idea of being able to help them.

Richard dropped them back at the Trekking Centre stables, where they had their own jobs to finish off. Danielle, the owner was there to greet them. "Welcome back girls!" she said. "Are you now fully knowledgeable and able to help the horses?" Ava, Skye and Gracie laughed. "Not quite!" smiled Skye. "But we are still very good at mucking out and doing the hay

Ava gets the head collar ready. Skye takes Barney back to his field.

Danielle helps Gracie and Ava.

bales," she laughed. Danielle laughed too and they all said goodbye to Richard and thanked him for the tour.

What an interesting day! The grown-ups were up to all sorts of things. Who would have thought there would be so many jobs? They wondered who would be next.

The end.

What do the grown-ups do?

The books are available in paperback through all good bookstores as well as through www.troubador.com and other places online. For more information, please check the website **www.kidseducationalbooks.com**.

The What do the grown-ups do? series in order of publication:

Book 1: Joe the Fisherman

Book 2: Papa the Stockfarmer

Book 3: Sean the Actor

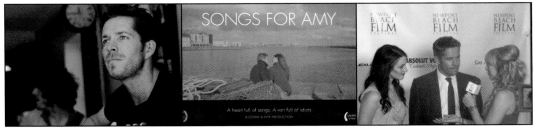

Book 4: Fiona the Doctor

Book 5: Richard the Vet

Book 6: Gordon the Wildlife Filmmaker

More coming soon!

What do the grown-ups do? series

The What do the grown-ups do? series is designed to teach children, aged 5-10 years, about different jobs. Based in the Highlands of Scotland, the stories are chatty and light-hearted, written through the eyes of the Mackenzie children as they meet real workers who explain their jobs.

Richard is a large animal vet. Specialising in equines (horses), he spends most of his time between farms and stables. His hours are long but he loves his job. On their adventure, the children learn how Richard helps farmers to manage their prize bulls, how horses' teeth never stop growing, how to remove rotten teeth and how to avoid getting kicked!

"What a refreshing an innovative way of introducing children to carer possibilities in later life. A delightful series of books, which gently guides younger children through the adult world of work."
Louise Webster, Broadcaster.

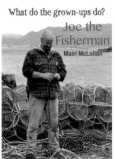

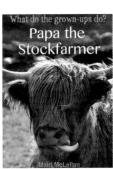

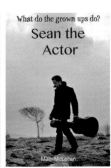

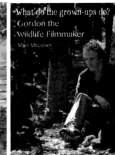